# Dragonfly

Kelly Borchelt

**KIDHAVEN PRESS**
*An imprint of Thomson Gale, a part of The Thomson Corporation*

EVANSTON PUBLIC LIBRARY
CHILDREN'S DEPARTMENT
1703 ORRINGTON AVENUE
EVANSTON, ILLINOIS 60201

**THOMSON**

**GALE**

Detroit • New York • San Francisco • San Diego • New Haven, Conn. • Waterville, Maine • London • Munich

© 2005 Thomson Gale, a part of The Thomson Corporation.

Thomson and Star Logo are trademarks and Gale and Kidhaven Press are registered trademarks used herein under license.

*For more information, contact*
Kidhaven Press
27500 Drake Rd.
Farmington Hills, MI 48331-3535
Or you can visit our Internet site at http://www.gale.com

**LIBRARY OF CONGRESS CATALOGING-IN-PUBLICATION DATA**

Borchelt, Kelly
  Dragonfly / by Kelly Borchelt.
    p. cm. — (Bugs)
Includes bibliographical references and index.
Summary: Describes the physical characteristics of dragonflies, their life cycle, where they live, and their eating habits.
  ISBN 0-7377-1770-x (hardback : alk. paper)
  1. Dragonfly—Juvenile literature. [1. Dragonfly.] I. Title. II. Series.

Printed in China

# CONTENTS

# Winged Wonders

There are over five thousand types of dragonflies found all over the world. More than four hundred kinds live in North America alone. Although they seem to look the same, like snowflakes, no two dragonflies are exactly alike. They come in many different colors and sizes. Even their wings are unique.

All dragonflies have a slim body made of three parts: a head, thorax, and abdomen. It is covered by a

**Opposite:** A dragonfly head is shown magnified many times its normal size.

**Dragonflies have colorful outer shells and delicate, veiny wings.**

protective shell that may appear blue, green, red, black, yellow, or even purple. Some dragonflies have a shell that shines with all the colors of the rainbow.

Like the dragonfly's body, its wings are often colorful and sparkle like diamonds in the sunlight. The wings get their color from a chemical called **pigment**. When sunlight touches the wings, blues, greens, and other colors shimmer.

The veins that carry blood to a dragonfly's wings are arranged in beautiful patterns. Like spiderwebs, each is different, varying from one dragonfly to another. Scientists use these patterns to tell dragonflies apart. The veins of some dragonflies' wings are far apart, while others are very close together. Sometimes the veins are packed together so tightly that it looks like the wings have spots.

The dragonfly's large compound eyes have thousands of tiny lenses that give the insect excellent vision.

## Little Dragons

Dragonflies can look a little scary. They are much larger than most insects and their big wings and long, spiny legs make them look like tiny dragons. That is why these amazing bugs are called dragonflies.

A dragonfly's head has two large eyes and a pair of tiny antennae. Each eye has ten thousand to twenty-five thousand **facets**, or lenses, that can turn different directions and see many images. Together these images form one detailed picture. These eyes provide the dragonfly with excellent vision.

The middle of a dragonfly's body is called the thorax. It supports three pairs of legs as well as the muscles that control the powerful wings. Each of the six legs is covered by two rows of spines and has a hooked claw on its tip for holding on to a perch or prey. The dragonfly's

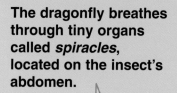

The dragonfly breathes through tiny organs called *spiracles*, located on the insect's abdomen.

Compound eyes have as many as twenty-five thousand lenses, and allow the dragonfly to see in many directions at one time.

Spiny, clawed legs allow the dragonfly to capture and hold prey.

Two pairs of powerful wings enable the dragonfly to hover in one place, or fly at speeds of up to sixty miles per hour.

needlelike abdomen holds its digestive and repro-ductive systems as well as its breathing organs, tiny holes called **spiracles**.

## Hovering Helicopters

Dragonflies have two pairs of strong wings with a wingspan that averages three to four inches. Unlike most insects with four wings, dragonflies can move their wings independently of each other. As one pair moves up, the other moves down, allowing the dragonfly to fly like a helicopter.

Dragonflies spend most of their adult lives in the air, stopping every now and then to mate, eat, or rest. A dragonfly may hover in one place or dart around at speeds of up to sixty miles per hour. Dragonflies can even fly backwards.

These special features make the dragonfly one of the most unique members of the insect world, but the dragonfly is not born with them. It spends most of its life growing into the strange creature humans see darting around ponds on a hot summer day.

# Life Changes

A dragonfly's life has three stages and lasts about one year. However, some have been known to live for several years. At least one dragonfly is known to have lived for five years.

In the first stage, a tiny egg is laid in or near fresh water. Dragonfly eggs are laid one by one or in large groups. They are so small that hundreds of them can be laid in the stem of a single plant. Sometimes the

*Opposite:* A male and female dragonfly mate. After mating, female dragonflies lay hundreds of eggs.

eggs are held snugly in place by thin threads that work like tiny boat anchors. Other times they are covered with a sticky coating and hang together in clumps like grapes. This stage usually lasts two to five weeks.

The second stage is the longest in a dragonfly's life. It begins when an egg hatches and a **nymph** crawls out. Most nymphs will

Dragonfly nymphs live underwater for several months (above) before they emerge as adults (left).

live underwater for several months before becoming adults. However, some have been known to stay under the water for many years. If the area where it hatched suddenly gets cold, the nymph will stay deep in the water until the weather warms up.

Nymphs look nothing like dragonflies. A newborn nymph is about the size of a grain of rice and its body is short and round. Nymphs are not very colorful. They are usually gray or brown. This dull color helps them blend into their surroundings.

As the nymph grows, its skin does not stretch, so it **molts**, or sheds its skin. The old skin will get hard and crack like an eggshell. The nymph crawls out in a new skin. A nymph will molt ten to fifteen times. After its third or fourth molt, tiny wing pads will appear on the nymph's thorax. These pads will be the dragonfly's wings.

In the third stage, the nymph is ready to become a dragonfly. It will wait until night, then

After its final molting, a dragonfly clings to its old skin and waits for its wings to dry.

Life Changes 13

crawl out of the water. The nymph will find a safe perch and then sit and wait.

## All Grown Up

During the night the nymph's skin will harden and split apart. As the skin cracks, a dragonfly will wiggle out. It will cling to its old skin until it can fly. The dragonfly cannot fly at first because its wings are moist and wrinkled like tiny, wet raisins.

A young dragonfly dries its wings in the sun.

As the sun rises, the wings will stretch and dry. Blood will flow through the veins in the wings and they will be full size by morning. Once its wings are dry, the dragonfly will zip off to hunt and mate.

A male dragonfly will first choose a territory and then fly around looking for a female. It will show off its most colorful parts and make a whirring sound with its wings to attract its mate.

After mating, the female will begin to lay eggs and the life cycle will start over. This last stage usually lasts only one month because dragonflies die shortly after reproducing. However, finding a mate may take a while, so the dragonfly makes itself at home in the sky.

A male dragonfly shows off its colorful body to attract a mate.

# At Home in the Air

**D**ragonflies can be found all over the world, except on the frozen continent of **Antarctica**. They prefer mild to warm weather and usually live near freshwater ponds, lakes, streams, or swamps. The dragonfly's main purpose in life is to mate, and these places are the best for laying its eggs.

Dragonflies are most active when the sun is out, so they do most of their hunting and mating during the day. Dragonflies stay busy zooming

**Opposite:** During the day, dragonflies are constantly on the go.

around in the air and will stop only now and then to rest or mate. Since they prefer the warmth of sunshine, they may seek shelter at night when it gets cool, or even if it gets cloudy. Dragonflies will gather in groups in a nearby bush or tree when they need shelter. Sometimes a dragonfly will even rest in the thick grasses of a nearby field.

Dragonflies stop long enough only to rest (below) or to mate (left).

A dragonfly's environment is very important because it is a **cold-blooded** creature. This means that its body temperature will fall in cold weather and rise in hot weather. If a dragonfly gets too cold, its body temperature will drop so low that it may not be able to move its wings. Dragonflies must be able to fly to escape predators, hunt for food, and find a mate. For this reason, they live in climates where they are less likely to get too cold.

Dragonflies prefer to be warm, but they will also avoid too much heat. When a dragonfly gets too hot, it will find a shady shelter and rest for a while until the weather cools. If it cannot find any shade, it will make its own using its wings like an umbrella.

## On the Go

Dragonflies do not build or live in permanent homes, such as a nest or hive. Instead, they flit about from one place to another around the body of water where they were laid as tiny eggs. They may return to the same spot on a

Because they are cold-blooded, dragonflies depend on the warmth of the sun to heat their bodies.

An emperor dragonfly rests on a blade of grass. Dragonflies rarely stay in one place for very long.

rock or plant over and over again, but they never stay there for very long.

Although a dragonfly will usually live out its short adult life in the same place where it hatched, it may fly off to find a new territory that is far away. It might leave to find a mate or more food. A dragonfly may also be driven away from its original territory by a change in the climate, or if too many humans move into the area.

This does not happen very often, but sometimes dragonflies gather in large groups and fly to a new territory, like birds **migrating** in the winter. In 1995 hundreds of dragonflies were seen crossing the choppy waters of the English Channel, migrating between England and Europe. Even today, no one knows just why all of those dragonflies suddenly needed to find a new home.

Although a dragonfly's main goal is to mate, it must also eat. Much of the time a dragonfly spends flying through the sky is spent hunting and eating.

# Dragonfly Dinners

Though they may vary by size and color, all dragonflies have one thing in common: a ferocious appetite. Dragonflies get plenty of exercise zipping about and looking for a mate, so they need to eat quite a bit to keep going and going.

Dragonflies are hungry from the moment they hatch as nymphs. Both nymphs and dragonflies are called **predators** because they hunt for living prey.

21

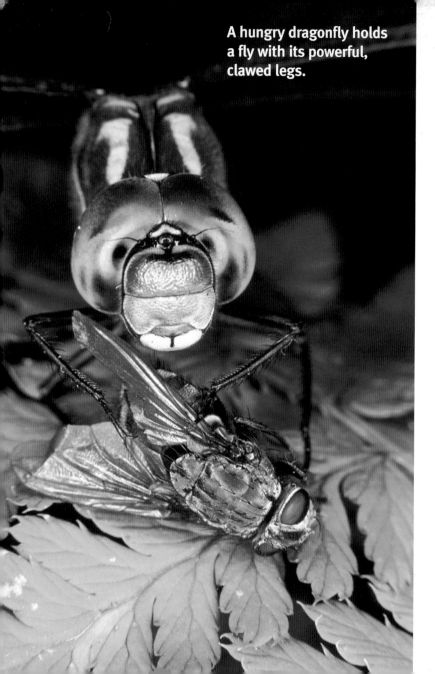

**A hungry dragonfly holds a fly with its powerful, clawed legs.**

As soon as it is hatched, a nymph will begin to eat its own egg yolk, but that only lasts for a short while. Soon, it will begin devouring whatever prey it can find. Nymphs prey on other small insects, tadpoles, shellfish, and even small fish. They are such vicious hunters that they are often called "water monsters."

A nymph will use its colorings as camouflage and wait for prey to come along. When the prey is within reach, the nymph will snatch it up by swinging out a special lip called a **labium**. This hinged lower lip may be up to half the length of the nymph's entire body. It is covered in tiny bristles and has sharp pincers that help the nymph grab onto its victim and pull it into its mouth.

The labium is also called a mask because it covers part of the nymph's face when it is not extended. Once the nymph has its prey, it will stuff it into its mouth and crush it with powerful jaws called **mandibles**.

In this magnified image, a dragonfly nymph extends its hinged lower lip, or labium, as its prey comes within reach.

## Neat Eaters

Adult dragonflies spend most of their short life eating. They will feed on other flying insects, such as mosquitoes, bees, flies, and gnats.

A dragonfly's large eyes and excellent vision are designed especially for hunting. It can see prey up to forty feet away. For a human, that would be like spotting an object the size of a baseball from across three football fields.

A dragonfly will hold its front legs together like a basket as its flies toward its prey. Then it will scoop up its meal and eat it in the air. Sometimes a dragonfly will simply open its mouth and fly through a swarm of insects, chomping them up as they gather in its jaws.

Although they may be vicious hunters, dragonflies are polite eaters. Whenever a dragonfly finishes a meal, it will first find a perch. Then it will use its legs to clean its face the same way a cat gives itself a bath with its paws.

Dragonflies are predators, but they are also prey. Creatures such as birds, snakes, frogs, and

*Opposite:* A hungry nymph devours a small fish with its powerful jaws.

Although they are fierce predators, dragonflies often fall prey to other creatures, such as this green frog.

spiders often make a tasty treat out of an unsuspecting dragonfly. Dragonflies depend on their flying skills and superior vision to protect them from these dangers. In cold weather, when a dragonfly cannot fly, it will raise its abdomen and flick its wings to scare away attackers.

Dragonflies are amazing creatures because of their many unique features and abilities. A dragonfly's brilliant colors, helicopter-like flying abilities, and excellent vision make it a great hunter and survivor in the insect world.

# GLOSSARY

Antarctica: The earth's southernmost continent.

cold-blooded: A creature whose body temperature varies with its environment.

facets: One side on an insect's compound eye.

labium: A nymph's lower lip, used for capturing prey.

mandibles: An insect's jaws.

migrating: To move from one place to another.

molt: To shed an outer skin.

nymph: The immature form of an insect.

pigment: The natural coloring of an animal or insect.

predator: An animal that hunts and eats other animals.

spiracles: Tiny breathing holes in an insect's abdomen.

# FOR FURTHER EXPLORATION

## Books

George Bernard, *Dragonflies*. New York: Putnam, 1980. A description of the physical characteristics and habits of dragonflies.

Emery Bernhard, *Dragonfly*. New York: Holiday House, 1993. An illustrated introduction to the physical characteristics, life cycle, and natural environment of dragonflies.

Molly McLaughlin, *Dragonflies*. New York: Walker, 1989. An illustrated description of a dragonfly's life cycle.

Cynthia Overbeck, *Dragonflies*. Minneapolis, MN: Lerner, 1982. An illustrated introduction to dragonflies and their three-stage life cycle.

## Web Sites

**Digital Dragonflies** (www.dragonflies.org). This site has many colorful pictures and information on several different types of dragonflies.

**Encyclopedia Encarta Article** (http://encarta.msn.com). This article describes the characteristics of dragonflies, and their development.

# INDEX

# PICTURE CREDITS

## ABOUT THE AUTHOR

Kelly Borchelt is a freelance writer who enjoys travel and research. She earned a bachelor's degree in marketing from Texas A&M University in Corpus Christi, Texas, and has been previously published with KidHaven. Borchelt resides on the Texas coast with her husband Preston and daughter Maylyn.